Yes, Virginia, There Is a Santa Claus

YES, VIRGINIA, THERE IS A SANTA CLAUS

BY FRANCIS PHARCELLUS CHURCH
FOREWORD BY CHRISTINE ALLISON
ILLUSTRATIONS BY THOMAS NAST

A John Boswell Associates Book
Delacorte Press

Published by Delacorte Press
Bantam Doubleday Dell Publishing Group, Inc.
666 Fifth Avenue
New York, New York 10103

Library of Congress Cataloging in Publication Data
  Church, Francis Pharcellus. 1839—1906.
    [Is there a Santa Claus?]
    Yes, Virginia, there is a Santa Claus / Francis Pharcellus Church:
    Introduction by Christine Allison.
          p.   cm.
    Summary: The text of the well-known editorial explaining that
    Santa Claus exists despite rumors to the contrary.
      ISBN 0-385-30854-X : $10.00
    1. Christmas—Juvenile literature. 2. Santa Claus—Juvenile
    literature. 3. O'Hanlon, Virginia—Juvenile literature.
    [1. Santa Claus. 2. Christmas.} I. O'Hanlon, Virginia. II. Title.
    GT4985.5.C53   1992
    394.2'68282—dc20   92-12268
                                                  CIP
                                                  AC
Text design by Nan Jernigan/The Colman Press
Manufactured in the United States of America
Published simultaneously in Canada

November 1992
10 9 8 7 6 5 4 3 2 1

DEDICATION

For Virginia Lea Marie Allison,
who asked

Foreword

For generations, children at the age of reason have asked a familiar question: "Is there a Santa Claus?" My daughter, who happens to be named Virginia, was no exception. Until the age of seven or eight, she and her school friends had been fairly certain of his existence, but then came the day that they discovered some "evidence" that made them question their childhood beliefs. Her friend Ben found some brand-new toys piled up in his mother's closet, and Ronan came upon some shopping bags in the basement. Virginia stumbled upon some packages in our garage (and got no more than a weak and clumsy explanation.) Against every wish in her heart, my daughter was beginning to believe that Santa might be a hoax.

And so she asked me, "Mom, is there a Santa Claus?" It was one of those questions that stops the world, and while Virginia's voice was defiant in a seven-year-old kind of way, her eyes said: Don't tell me Mom.

A thought rushed into my head. In reply, I said to my daughter, "Did you know that there was once another little girl named Virginia who asked her parents if Santa is real? She put her question to the editor of a famous newspaper, and the answer is treasured all over the world. I'll find the story for you, and we'll read it together."

I had a vague recollection of the editorial, but I was unprepared for the magic I'd find in the pages of a crumbling newspaper nearly a hundred years old. For in that editor's wonderful reply lies an answer that has beguiled and informed the hearts of millions.

Virginia O'Hanlon's letter and Mr. Francis Pharcellus Church's response are reprinted here as they appeared in *The New York Sun* on September 21, 1897.

Merry Christmas.

— Christine Allison

S THERE A SANTA CLAUS?

WE TAKE pleasure in answering at once and thus prominently the communication below expressing at the same time our great gratification that its faithful author is numbered among the friends of *The Sun:*

Dear Editor:

I am eight years old. Some of my little friends say there is no Santa Claus.

Papa says, "If you see it in The Sun *it's so."*

Please tell me the truth, is there a Santa Claus?

VIRGINIA O'HANLON
115 WEST 95TH STREET

IRGINIA, your little friends are wrong. They have been affected by the skepticism of a skeptical age. They do not believe except they see. They think that nothing can be which is not comprehensible by their little minds. All minds, Virginia, whether they be men's or children's, are little. In this great universe of ours man is a mere insect, an ant, in his intellect, as compared with the boundless world about him, as measured by the intelligence capable of grasping the whole of truth and knowledge.

YES, VIRGINIA, there is a Santa Claus. He exists as certainly as love and generosity and devotion exist, and you know that they abound and give to your life its highest beauty and joy. Alas, how dreary would be the world if there were no Santa Claus! It would be as dreary as if there were no Virginias. There would be no childlike faith then, no poetry, no romance to make tolerable this existence. We should have no enjoyment, except in sense and sight. The eternal light with which childhood fills the world would be extinguished.

NOT BELIEVE in Santa Claus! You might as well not believe in fairies! You might get your papa to hire men to watch in all the chimneys on Christmas Eve to catch Santa Claus coming down, but what would that prove? Nobody sees Santa Claus, but that is no sign that there is no Santa Claus. The most real things in the world are those that neither children nor men can see. Did you ever see fairies dancing on the lawn? Of course not, but that's no proof that they are not there. Nobody can conceive or imagine all of the wonders there are unseen and unseeable in the world.

YOU TEAR apart a baby's rattle and see what makes the noise inside, but there is a veil covering the unseen world which not the strongest man, nor the united strength of all the strongest men that ever lived, could tear apart. Only faith, fancy, poetry, love, romance can push aside that curtain and view and picture the supernal beauty and glory beyond. Is it all real? Ah, Virginia, in this world there is nothing else real and abiding.

No Santa Claus! Thank God he lives, and lives forever. A thousand years from now, Virginia, nay ten times ten thousand years from now, he will continue to make glad the heart of childhood.

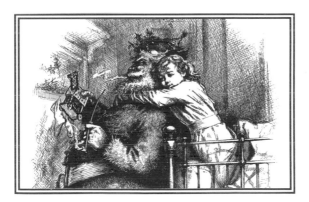

Virginia O'Hanlon

Even in these days of rather precocious children, a letter to an editor of a major newspaper from an eight-year-old would certainly give one pause. Yet Virginia O'Hanlon wrote just such a letter as the nineteenth century was drawing to a close, unusual on the face of it, and highly unusual in that she was a little girl. It was at her father's urging that Virginia turned to the editor of *The New York Sun* with one of the most famous questions of all time.

She was not an ordinary child, and she became an extraordinary woman. After growing up on the Upper West Side of New York City she is said to have received a bachelor's degree from Hunter College in 1910 and then a master's degree from Columbia University in 1911.

Miss O'Hanlon married, and it is somehow not surprising that she devoted her life to teaching and working with children who were chronically ill.

Francis P. Church

When the curmudgeonly Francis Pharcellus Church, an editor at *The New York Sun,* was handed Virginia O'Hanlon's letter and told to write a response for the next day's edition, he was an unlikely choice for the assignment.

"At first he bristled and pooh-poohed the subject," Edward P. Mitchell, his editor, wrote later, " but took the letter and turned with an air of resignation to his desk." Church dashed off his legendary editorial in a very short time, and in doing so struck a glancing blow to skeptics of every era.

One wonders if Church was a religious man, for his eloquent text suggests such a keen grasp of the mystery of faith. It is hard to say, but he was the son of a distinguished clergyman and journalist. Journalism ran in the family: His father, Pharcellus Church, founded the old *New York Chronicle* and both Francis and his brother, William Conant, were newspapermen.

During the Civil War, Francis Church was a war correspondent for *The New York Times*. After the war, he and his brother established *The Army and Navy Journal,* and then *Galaxy Magazine*, which merged with *Atlantic Monthly*. Francis Church then took a post as an editorial writer for *The New York Sun*, where he was to write "Is There a Santa Claus?"

"Is There a Santa Claus?" was written in a rational age, when most people were confident that science, with all of its new discoveries and methods, would provide all the answers. It is worth noting that this answer, affirming the existence of Santa Claus, has outlived most of the scientific and quasi-scientific theories of that day.

It was not until after his death in 1906 that it became publicly known that Church had written the reply to Virginia O'Hanlon.

Thomas Nast

The man who wills himself down chimneys and into the hearts of children did not always look so fat and jolly. It was Thomas Nast, a political cartoonist for *Harper's Weekly*, who gave Santa Claus his ample flesh and cheery red cheeks.

Before Nast, most children in the United States envisioned Santa as a Dutch figure, Sinterklaas, who wore pantaloons and pilgrim shoes — a somewhat unattractive fellow with a large nose. In 1862, Nast published the first image of Santa as we know him: the kindly man with the long white beard, rosy red cheeks, and big belly.

Nast was influenced by two images: the gnomelike German Santa of his childhood, Pelez-Nichol, and the Santa described in Clement C. Moore's poem, "A Visit from St. Nicholas." It was Moore who put pounds on Santa: the stomach that shook like a bowl full of jelly was entirely the poet's innovation as were the eight tiny reindeer. Nast layered on his own touches, the most important of which was Santa's homeland of the North Pole: a cold, hard-to-reach place that had no real nationality.

Each year, Nast published Christmas cartoons for *Harper's Weekly*, and many of them featured Santa ministering to the families torn by the Civil War. They were powerful, poignant images that soothed a nation. Though Nast is best known to historians for his assaults on the corrupt Tweed Ring of New York City, it was his collection of Santa Claus drawings that he is said to have treasured most.

Acknowledgments

Emily Reichert said yes, the world should have this essay again. Nan Jernigan made it beautiful, and Patty Brown and John Boswell made it reality. Special thanks to the staff at the Larchmont Public Library for their patience and assistance.

Credits

Thomas Nast's Santa Claus illustrations and the biographical information on Nast came from *Christmas Drawings for the Human Race,* by Thomas Nast. The text is reprinted from the original September 21, 1897, edition of *The New York Sun.*